T0132366

Legend

of

Pigeon
Roost
Road

Legend

of

Pigeon
Roost
Road

Frances A. Wood

iUniverse, Inc.
New York   Bloomington

Legend of Pigeon Roost Road

iUniverse books may be ordered through booksellers or by contacting:

iUniverse
1663 Liberty Drive
Bloomington, IN 47403
www.iuniverse.com
1-800-Authors (1-800-288-4677)

ISBN: 978-1-4401-8913-5 (pbk)
ISBN: 978-1-4401-8914-2 (ebk)

Printed in the United States of America

iUniverse rev. date: 12/3/2009

Dedication

For the most part this book is dedicated to my one and only son, his father, in memory of Robert Wood.

Robert Wood was Cliff's best friend and gave his life in the Navy in World War II.

This book is also dedicated to some of the happiest times in my life with my son whom I have spent my life just being grateful that I was his mother. It is also dedicated to my husband who was my guardian angel for twenty nine years. My son gave his life to Jesus when he was nine years old and I was twenty nine. We were baptized together.

Also there were many others in my life that were important to help me succeed at a time when times were hard. My parents were there if I needed them and my many wonderful friends. My supervisors in the many places where I worked were all good people. I was short on relatives and lived my life without them.

My family was on the move a lot and my education today is because of the change of scenery and smart people that I was associated with.

Tommy seemed to thrive on the diversified experiences in our lives. He was self educated in many fields like electronics, radio, communications and science. He never attended a four year college and yet he retired from Philips Magnavox, Inc, and worked as an application engineer. The Silicon Valley was pure heaven to my son.

Also I am grateful to Cliff Walker for the inspiration he gave me to write books.

Cliff teaches a creative writing class and is very supportive of my books. Also my friend Oran Pearson helped me on the computer when I was new at it.

Frances A. Wood

Introduction

This book is the life story of the years as we lived on the Pigeon Roost Road. The time passed quickly and we were not prepared for all the mysteries that took place in that time of our lives. It was an education for my husband, my son and me. Tommy, my son, spent his formative years experiencing the mysteries along with Cliff, my husband, and myself while living on the Pigeon Roost Road.

The book is truly a legend and will live on in the memory of all who came in contact with us during this period of our lives.

Contents

chapter one

First Look

When I first heard of this rare spot on the face of this earth I was anxious to know more about how it got its name. Upon close inspection I discovered it was a short half circle of paved road and connecting to the main highway into town. It was a part of an old road that was primarily the main thoroughfare. The name had remained for many years. I was never able to research the Pigeon Roost Road properly, but it could well have been there when the Cherokee Indians were in that vicinity.

My husband had met an associate at work and had been informed that a house and five acres were for sale, on the Pigeon Roost Road. We drove out to inspect the property and found it to be very undesirable, but at the same time it was very intriguing at first sight. We did a walk through inspection. Apparently no one had lived there for many years. It needed lots of paint and many repairs plus some care and concern. We were young, ambitious and both in good health, so we looked farther.

We went inside to find an antique upright piano in the front room. As we continued through the house we spotted another antique, an electric cook stove in the kitchen. An unusual thing was a pull down stairway to the attic. All in working order. I noticed that there were lots of windows in the house to let in plenty of light. A locked door led to the basement. Most old houses had a basement. The master bedroom had an adjoining small room. This could be perfect for our three year old Tommy.

I was beginning to see the possibilities of this old dilapidated and run down place, to restore it and make a livable home.

We stepped outside again and three big apple trees were loaded with fruit. The air was fresh, the sun was warm and the stillness compared to the city it was refreshing.

We were newly married and living in a two room apartment in a busy part of town with no place for a three year old to run and play. There were eight more apartments in the building and a lot of kids.

My husband was anxious to experiment his ideas of farming and he seemed to want to buy this place. The cost was affordable and the mortgage could be a 100% G.I. Loan. We would only have to rake up the closing costs.

We decided to buy the place and applied for the loan. It was approved and was so easy to just move in. Our work was laid out for us and we started on the front porch. The screen was rusty and we removed that and painted the porch. It made such a difference that we thought what next? One bad feature was the shingle roof and we could do nothing about that. They are fire hazards. The roof went with the house so we accepted it.

The next big project was a backyard fence. We bought the wire, nails and the posts and did the work ourselves. So now little Tommy could play outside. I could get more work done. New curtains made a big difference in the looks of the interior. Cliff invested in a new sewing machine from Sears. So then I could make curtains and drapes for the whole house. The new machine would be paying off for a long time to come. I made my clothes and shirts for Cliff and Tommy. I made a coat for myself. As time went by we got some living room furniture and I made slip covers for the divan and chairs.

A mule was purchased by Cliff and we found out later that the mule was moon eyed and could only see certain times of the month. Not only was he disabled but he was old and died the first winter.

I looked out the kitchen window and got the scare of my life when I saw my baby standing outside the fence and under this blind mule. If he had moved he would have stepped on my baby. I did recover Tommy, led him to the yard and locked the gate.

My husband got a plow and used that mule to break some ground for a garden. Cliff did not listen to me about planting the garden. The whole spot was planted. In time the seeds sprouted and the corn never got more than four inches tall. The beans grew but were a pale green. It was all a waste of time because you cannot grow vegetables without fertilizer. It was evident that we needed fertilizer. So Cliff was not to be outdone and showed up with a truckload of cottonseed hulls and covered the whole area. He then plowed the fertilizer under and we planted a crop of potatoes. The seed potatoes came from some discarded produce that Cliff got from a super market in town. You cut the eyes of the potato and plant them. After the potato crop which was very successful we had a garden spot that would grow anything.

I bought a canner and could can all the apples, wild plums, berries and any fruits and vegetables that we had access to. My canner was a cold pack and I could can eight quart jars at a time. We grew so many tomatoes, green beans, squash and beets in our garden that Cliff was taking them to work and selling to his fellow workers. I never owned a pressure cooker canner as I was afraid of them.

We planted vegetables that produced on top of the ground by the light of the moon and all those vegetables that produced under ground by the dark of the moon. It was just an old wives tale but seemed to work for us. The veggies grew mainly because our soil was so rich.

Our neighbors across the road were Annie and Lawrence. Their house had a cistern to catch the rainwater. Their house had a large oaken pail at the foot of the cistern and they had planted some small fish in the pail. Annie showed me how she caught the fish and cooked them for her dinner.

Lawrence was always ready to assist Cliff when he wanted to butcher a hog or make a trip to the grist mill.

Our neighbor down the road was Cliff's associate worker and he had twenty acres and some horses, a wife and seven kids.

One day I was in the yard and happened to spot a fire or black smoke in the direction of our neighbors' house. Sure enough it looked as though their house was on fire. Cliff and I ran through the field to see if we could help. By the time we got there it was too late to extinguish the flames. The men reached through an open window and pulled a sewing machine out and it was not burned. After the fire and everything was cold they cleaned up the spot and later built another house. The immediate problem was to find a place for two adults and seven kids to live. They borrowed a house trailer from a friend. The new house was modern and nicer than the one that burned.

chapter two

Turkey for Thanksgiving

I have not mentioned before but Cliff got carried away when we bought our house and bought twenty baby turkeys without knowing how difficult they were to raise. A bet was made with some man that he could raise eighteen of the turkeys. They did well as long as they were in the brooder but when they were transferred to a wire bottom cage they began to die. They must have had some horrible turkey disease that spread from one turkey to another. When the remaining five were left, Cliff opened the cage door and let them go free. After that we could see our turkeys roaming the fields and living off the seeds and water they could find. There was one gobbler and four hens.

The Turkeys in the pen

Those turkeys went everywhere. One day we went to get feed for the pigs that Cliff was raising. He planned to raise the pigs to maturity and butcher one and breed the other one. Well, we came home to find one pig had a skin in his mouth that looked a lot like a turkey leg. We looked around and spotted only three turkeys. Just one turkey gobbler and two hens. The two missing turkeys were eaten by the pigs.

Thanksgiving was a month away. There was just time enough to purchase fifty dollars worth of raffle tickets and sell them for turkey prizes. It went well with the gobbler as first prize. Second prize was of course the hen turkey. That left the one that Cliff was going to give to the man who made the silly bet. It was unlawful to bet and a cardinal sin to boot. So we kept the remaining turkey for our own Thanksgiving dinner.

The weather turned very cold after Thanksgiving and we decided to kill one of the pigs. They had grown into hogs by that time.

Cliff went across the road and got Lawrence to help him to kill the hog. It was a big job and required a lot of help. My mother was there at the time and could give us a lot of information about the meat and how to make good sausage. It was understood that Lawrence would take home the head, feet and chitterlings.

Our neighbor, Roy, took home some of the meat. We had no freezer to keep the meat so had to use our refrigerator. We cured the hams and shoulders. I learned to make crackling bread which was the fatty parts of the hog's insides and cooked in the cornbread.

The weather got cold after Thanksgiving and in December we butchered one of the pigs. It wasn't a pig anymore. They call them hogs when they get grown. We got Lawrence from across the road to come over and kill the hog and butcher it. It was a big job and required a lot of help. Of course Lawrence would take home the feet, head and chitterlings. There were two hams, two shoulders, ribs, roast, tenderloin and bacon or side meat. There was plenty for sausage. My mother was there to help and she had grown up on a farm. So she knew what to do with the meat.

It wasn't three weeks until we had a bad storm with some freezing weather. The ground was covered with snow. The hog we planned to breed was at our neighbors place and slipped on the ice and broke a hip. The neighbor called and said that before fever sets in the only thing to do was to butcher the hog without delay. There had to be another trip to get help to butcher the hog. Cliff went immediately in search of Lawrence.

It just happened that Lawrence was available and the three men worked in cold weather to get the job done. They made a fire which helped.

Now we had a problem with more meat than we could handle. Cliff solved the problem by selling the meat to his friends at work. It all worked out without losing our profit on the hogs.

chapter three

Tommy's Bird Dog

We were so busy with our adventures on the Pigeon Roost Road fixing, building and painting and one day Cliff brought home a bird dog puppy for Tommy. It was a German short haired pointer. Tommy would get up in the morning and before breakfast he would go outside to hold Rex in his arms, it was such a joy to see Tommy and his dog together until Rex reached the age of maturity.

As Rex grew to be a grown dog, Tommy was growing up, too. They were inseparable. Then one day a man came to see Rex and he was a hunter. He was so attracted to the dog. Cliff took Rex for a walk to the back of the property and he came upon a flock of birds and made a beautiful point. The man offered $75.00 for Tommy's dog. Rex was sold and Cliff promised Tommy another dog.

We began to feed a stray dog and he hung around. He was a red chow and very friendly. One day he disappeared and we looked for him to come back. We saw him lying in the weeds in the yard next door. We called to him and he would not come to us. Cliff decided to put him out of his misery and grabbed the shot gun. I got Tommy and we waited in the house for the shot. When we heard the shot we went outside and there was no dog in sight. Cliff had missed and the dog ran under the house. He would not come out to eat for five days. Later he came out and ate some food. The man across the road had shot the dog to keep him from catching his chickens. I wondered why because he never bothered our chickens. Soon the dog disappeared and we thought he may have been shot again by the man across the road.

Surprise, Cliff brought a pair of grown beagle hounds to Tommy. We did not know anything about beagles. Tommy soon found out that if he ran the beagles would chase him and bay and this became an everyday practice. It was alright to do this if Cliff was not sleeping.

Time passed and one day the female beagle presented us with nine puppies. Tommy was delighted and we named all nine of them. One puppy had a heart on his body and he was named Valentine. The puppies grew fast and soon Tommy ran around the house with all eleven beagles in chase and baying at a deafening racket. It woke up Cliff and Tommy got reprimanded for that.

There seemed to be a lot of work to do to improve our Pigeon Roost Road estate and we never got caught up.

Some livestock found their way into our garden one day because we did not have our property fenced. We could not afford to buy the fence posts that it would take to enclose our entire property. But there was a way.

Cliff worked for the Memphis Street Car Company. They were in the process of changing the street cars to all buses. Since the street cars ran on rails there were cross ties to be discarded. Cliff asked for enough cross ties to fence our property. He was granted the ties just for removing them.

We hauled 90 ties from the city of Memphis to our estate in a pickup truck. We made about 10 trips of 30 miles each way to retrieve the ties. This was a big job, but we had to do it. We did not complain of the blood, sweat and tears that we shed as we loaded each truck load of heavy ties. Then the fun began.

We purchased barbed wire enough to stretch three strands around the five acres that we owned. It was another big job to dig holes for each of the ties. As Cliff stretched the wire I nailed the wire to the posts with big staples.

As I look back now on this project, it seems almost impossible that we could undertake such an impossible task. I won't say how long it took to complete the fencing but when it was over, we looked with pride at our estate.

Cliff was not satisfied until he constructed a small barn. I thought how can we do this? Cliff drew the plans and of course we did not have a lot of money to spend but there was a way. We had the time and energy to start. There was a lumber mill just across the Tennessee border and the lumber was cheaper than it was in the big city of Memphis. We started by buying oak two by fours to construct the frame. We used motor oil to dip the nails in before we nailed them into the oak lumber.

The barn was taking shape and was to be what we needed for the cows and mule. The center portion of the barn was where we would store the hay for the animals. We constructed a wood floor in this section. Then on the side we extended the roof and sides for the milking stalls. We roofed the barn with tar paper on the roof as this was the cheapest way. We extended the driveway out to the barn so we could drive the truck right up to the barn.

Cliff was thinking of the comfort of the cows when he laid straw in the bottom of the stalls for the cows to stand on as they were milked.

A line fence between the garden spot and the barn was needed so the livestock could not get to the garden area where the house was located.

Cliff was a horse trader so if he could not sell an animal he just traded it for another one and that was how we got the rabbit mule, as we called it. The old moon-eyed mule had fallen in a ditch one night and could not get up. The poor thing just lay there and died. We found it the next morning.

The rabbit mule was not what we needed. When he was hitched up to a plow he suddenly decided to run away. He pulled Cliff and the plow about fifteen feet and Cliff was nearly beheaded by the blade of the plow before he was able to stop the mule.

One evening after Cliff had gone to work, I saw the mule straddle the fence and the barbed wire was cutting into his side. So I took some wire cutters and cut the barbed wire so he could get back into the yard.

I never trusted any mule because they can whirl around and kick you in a moment's notice. He never did this and I was ready to run if he tried it.

Not all the animals that Cliff brought home were useless. He brought home a cow and she gave us lots of rich milk. We had more milk than we needed so one of our neighbors bought a gallon a day from us.

Cliff's grandfather owned a dairy and Cliff just knew how to milk cows. I never learned to do this. To churn the milk and make butter was a new thing for me to learn. We did not have a churn and I found that storing milk in a fruit jar and shaking it would produce some butter. It was not much fun shaking the fruit jar so we bought a churn. Actually, we churned the cream. Rich milk always has a lot of cream.

Cliff liked to hunt and once he shot a raccoon and brought it to me. I suppose we ate the meat but a friend was studying to be a taxidermist. He stuffed that raccoon for me and because he did not have a license to do so he would not take any money. I paid him for the materials he used. It looked so real and was quite a conversational piece until it ended up in the attic.

Our water came from a well with an electric pump to furnish water inside the house. The well was 275 feet deep. One time I had a large carbuncle on the calf of my leg. It was so painful that I had to keep it elevated as it throbbed when it was not elevated. When the carbuncle finally ruptured there were seven heads. When it was well it left a hole in my leg. We must have had iron rust in our system.

Tommy had measles, chicken pox, whooping cough and scarlet fever before he started to school and grew up with a weak heart. He was stricken with rheumatic fever as a result of the many diseases; he could not run and play baseball without losing his breath.

The house next door to us was rented to a family with three kids. So now Tommy had somebody to play with. Every day the kids played together. Little Howard was Tommy's favorite. They climbed trees and shared their toys. There was a lady taking care of the children.

One day she came over to tell me there was a snake in her kitchen. She wanted help. I did not know what I could do but I went to her house and the snake was coiled in the corner of the room. I waved my apron and the snake saw the movement and crawled back into the hole in the floor. I said to the lady to stop up the hole so the snake could not return. I had seen so many snakes on the Pigeon Roost Road that I had conquered my greatest phobia of snakes.

Our first car, when we moved to the country, happened to be a piece of junk. Cliff did not have enough money to buy a new car. It was a little bit better than walking. It took a contortionist to drive it. You had to reach out the window and work the windshield wiper blades if it rained and steer the car with the other hand. The horn would not blow. If the car would not start you had to raise the hood and tap on the battery cable to get the car to start. After driving that car I was a real basket case. One day I drove the car just down the road to the feed store and when I came out of the feed store there was a flatbed truck parked next to me. I backed out of the parking place and cut the wheel so that the car sort of went under the bed of the truck. Very suddenly the fender on my car was ripped like a giant can opener had opened up the fender. That did it. Cliff went in search of another car. I was so sorry that we had to part with that prized possession. It was such a joy to drive that car.

Our next car happened to be a G.I. truck. It was a real iron pony. Only two seats and Tommy had to stand up if we all three went anywhere. There were no windows or doors and no keys. It had just a switch to turn on to start the motor. The truck never failed to start and we managed to do great things to improve our property.

Later we were all three driving home from town and it was raining very hard. We turned off the main highway onto the Pigeon Roost Road. To our sudden surprise the little creek was flooded. The small bridge railing was covered with the flood water. To go back on the highway and go around the creek would have been miles out of the way.

Cliff said "Hang on" and proceeded to cross the bridge. The water was inside of the truck as we crossed the bridge. The motor of the truck was churning away. Our feet were wet but we had crossed the bridge safely.

I did not have a driver's license and I had to learn to drive the truck to pass the test. I learned to double clutch, back up and turn around on a dime. Then I went into town for my license. The instructor at the DMV was amazed at my driving skills. He passed me and said you don't have to worry about anyone running into you. We never had an accident and never received a traffic citation.

One night or early morning Cliff was coming home in the truck. He called me and said someone has stolen the truck. I said well report it. He said OK and hung up. The next thing I knew he drove up in the driveway at home. His explanation was that one of his associates at work had played a trick on him and driven the truck around the corner of the block.

One more new experience for us was when Cliff went gigging for frogs. He came home with a big batch of frogs to be cleaned. We put the legs in a skillet and began to fry them and guess what? They actually jumped out of the pan. We put them back in the pan and finished cooking them. Good eating. The problem was to dispose of the remains of the frogs. If left for days and the smell can be horrendous.

Tommy's first puppy, Rex

Tommy and Rex

chapter four

A Snake in the Bedroom

This story was truly a miracle. One evening just before Cliff was to leave for work he had a few minutes to play marbles with Tommy. We were in the bedroom and one of the marbles rolled under the chest of drawers. So Cliff took the drawer out to reach under the furniture and to retrieve the marble. Instantly he saw a snake and quickly went to get an axe and a broom stick. While Tommy and I watched he used the broomstick to get the snake to crawl out into the open. We breathlessly watched as the snakes' head was crushed by the blunt end of the ax. Cliff left for work after disposing of the dead snake for the night.

The snake had been a two foot copperhead and as deadly poisonous as a rattlesnake only it had no rattles. You can bet we said our prayers that night before we went to sleep. Tomorrow was another day. We soon learned that we were not the only inhabitants of the Pigeon Roost Road estate. Apparently it had been a breeding ground for many years of very poisonous snakes. Some were copperheads. They were copper in color and about eighteen inches long and were as poisonous as the rattlesnakes of the west. They had no rattles to warn you. Also there were water moccasins and lived in the water holes.

We never unlocked the basement door. We knew that rainwater leaked into the basement walls. Nothing was ever done about it. Who knows it could have been full of snakes. As you will read later in this book that I became ill. I did however, overcome my phobia of snakes. As a child I would become frantic at the very sight of any snake.

We lived two miles from the town of White Haven and five miles from the city of Memphis. So we therefore, attended church services at White Haven. We were five miles from the city of Memphis. It was closer to attend church service at the small town.

There were stores, gas stations and people living in the town of Whitehaven.

A member of the church seemed to own the town. He had the general store and the gas station. This man became an acquaintance. We were all eager to save souls.

One night we joined a group of Christians to visit a lady of the church who lived alone and was troubled about her relationship with God. Little did we know what would happen when we visited her in her home? The house was lovely. It was a two story and the rooms were spacious. She met us at the door. She invited us to enter and gave us a tour all through the house and we retired to the living room. Eventually the conversation turned to religion.

We talked about Jesus and his life on earth. Jesus was crucified two thousand years ago and died on the cross to save us from our personal sins and promised us eternal life in heaven. In my father's house there are many mansions he said I will go to prepare a place for you and I will come again and receive you unto myself.

The hostess began to cry and seemed to be depressed and bewildered but at the same time she welcomed our company. We joined hands and prayed for her salvation. The leader of our group asked the lady if she would accept Jesus as her savior. She cried again and said yes she did accept Him.

I looked for the lady in church but never saw her again. As long as we lived at the Pigeon Roost Road estate I suppose that Cliff would be showing up with a new animal to feed. This time it was a Doberman pinscher a dark short haired, long legged dog with a touch of brown hair and a breed of terrier. Her name was Judy and she was trained to be a guard dog. What in the world was Cliff trying to do. Judy never liked me, in fact, she was jealous of any contact I had with my husband. One evening after Cliff had gone to work I opened the back door and to my surprise Judy was crouching and showing her teeth at me. Very quickly, I stamped my foot and said "Get out of here". To my surprise she obeyed me. But I did not trust her after that. It was not my intention to do anything about Cliff's dog but at the same time I did not want her around.

One morning Cliff went to feed Judy and found her unconscious. When she was taken to the vet the diagnosis was strychnine poisoning. We learned that strychnine is very poisonous, a colorless compound and has no taste. The vet took good care of Judy and she recovered.

The recovery for Judy did not last long for the person that wanted her dead struck again and with arsenic. The vet could not save her the second time because her intestines could not stand the deadly arsenic

chapter five

Uncle Hardy

My uncle Hardy showed up one day quite unexpectedly. He had lost his wife and was in search of his only sister, Julia, my mother.

He was a very religious man and proceeded to get us in line by having prayer meeting every night. He had me pegged as a Jezebel from the start. We humored him because he could tell us a lot of farming secrets. He made a hit with Tommy because Tommy followed him all over the place. Uncle Hardy told good stories that Tommy liked to hear. He only stayed a week and went back to his home in Texas. Before he left he bought me a bushel of peaches to can. When he returned home he joined the lonely hearts club and met a lady in Nashville, Tennessee. He married the lonely widow. She had a two story home and Uncle Hardy was a good handy man. They got along good together for many years.

Poor Uncle Hardy was getting up in age and he died of a massive heart attack. This was a blow to my mother as it happened just after my father had died of cancer. She felt insecure without the men in her life. I could not seem to comfort her. Time passed and she became both secure and independent. She lived 25 more years in California.

When we first moved in the house on the Pigeon Roost Road I mentioned some apple trees. Well they bore fruit each year and the apples were perfect for making apple pies, also the peelings were good to make apple juice. When the apple juice was mixed with peaches, berry or grape juice it formed an ingredient called pectin. This was necessary to make jelly. No need to run to the store and buy pectin.

We also went to the surrounding fields and picked wild plums. They were the size of marbles. We did not make many trips to the grocery store except for staples and then we stocked up on them. I canned so much that at one time I had seventy two quarts of tomatoes, fifty quarts of green beans. I tried once to can some cauliflower from the discarded produce that Cliff brought home. I just could not see food go to waste. We salvaged lemons, oranges, potatoes, apples, carrots and all were perfectly good with not a spot on them. If we are ever plagued with a famine I will remember those days when we had so much food.

Another source of materials that Cliff had was the army bases. They had crates of lumber that they called pallets. We hauled them away in our truck and the lumber was used to construct our pump house, chicken house and part of the barn. Maybe a dog house or two we built.

One trouble spot was our driveway. The original owners had cut a driveway from the road through the rough terrain and left the raw dirt. When it rained there was a possibility of getting stuck in the mud. So Cliff got busy on that problem.

This brings to mind a wise old saying that it's not the problem you have but what you do about it that counts. Cliff was good at finding a way. I certainly could not find a solution to this problem.

So in a few days Cliff brought home from a steel mill cinders that he got for free and spread them over the driveway. They looked just awful and in time the cinders packed down and the driveway began to take on the resemblance of a paved road.

I found a little cedar tree on the property and Cliff dug it up for me. We planted it by the house. Someone said that when the tree grew tall enough to shade my grave I would die. This was an old wives tale or a southern superstition to disturb your way of thinking. I did not believe the old wives tale and it proved to be wrong.

We could not afford to paint the outside of the house but we managed to paint the inside room by room. I stayed up late at night after Tommy was asleep and Cliff was at work to paint. By morning the paint would be dry. Tommy's room needed curtains so I made them out of the feed sacks. I used the plain sacks and traced cartoon figures on the material. I colored them with small crayons and then set the color with a hot iron over the wax paper. They could then be washed without losing the color. My mother visited me sometime and once while she was there we got up early and went to pick some berries. When we returned to the house Tommy was out of bed and had hurt his hand. He had tried to bandage it as well as a five year old could do. All it needed was a band aid. Tommy was OK and we were relieved.

chapter six

My Sewing Machine

At last Cliff bought me a sewing machine and it was a big help to make the shirts, dresses and curtains for the house. We got chicken feed in printed sacks and all the ladies were using them to make clothes. We had shirts, blouses and even dresses made from the feed sacks.

Tommy was very inquisitive about bugs. I guess all little boys go through this stage. He came screaming into the house one day. He was so upset because he had found a wasp nest and been stung several times. My antidote for stings was vinegar and soda. It sets up a foaming action and draws the poison right out. So Tommy was feeling OK in a short time.

Another time I had a bed of tulips in full bloom and they were all different colors. So pretty and I ask Tommy not to pick the tulips. So he went outside and in a few minutes he was back inside crying because a bee inside the tulip had stung him on the hand as he reached in for the bee. Now guess what? Tommy got another dose of baking soda and vinegar on his bee sting.

We learned that the Johnsons, that we bought our house from, had two aunts that lived in the house we bought. The piano and the antique stove had belonged to them. When the aunts passed on the house was sold to us. The Johnsons lived in a house next door to us and had a new house built across the way. The house next to us became a rental.

Cliff and Tommy and me

Tommy had tonsillitis when he was about five years old. The doctor advised us to have his tonsils removed before he began school. We did have the tonsillectomy performed. I stayed overnight in his room at the hospital.

Tommy was six years old in August and the next month he started school. He caught a school bus in front of our house on the Pigeon Roost Road.

He did well in school that year and passed to the second grade. In the middle of the term I became seriously ill.

Cliff and Tommy

chapter seven

Strange Illness

Cliff came home after he had worked all night. I had put Tommy to bed. It had been snowing outside and covering the ground very rapidly. About the first of December the weather began to get cold. I dressed for bed and for some odd reason instead of going to bed I walked outside in the snow barefoot and became very cold. I remember walking without my shoes to an old barn in the field.

When Cliff came home he found me in a state of shock. I did not know him and my mind was a blank. I could not remember what had happened. Cliff was very confused. He made a fire as the house was cold. I was wrapped in a blanket and my body was so cold. I was out of it and Cliff was at a loss as to what had happened during the night. What really happened was a mystery.

Finally daylight came and it was late enough to make phone calls. So Cliff called his sister first because she had been seeing a psychiatrist. She gave him the phone number and he called the doctor. Cliff made arrangements to take me to see that doctor.

I was placed in a sanitarium for thirty days. We had no medical insurance and the expense was unbearable. I was aware that I was being led around by the nurse. My bath water was prepared for me and I was led back to the room and locked in. I could not relate to so many strangers. After about thirty days I could not see any one and I looked out an upstairs window and saw people in cars in the parking lot.

I walked around the room and finally sat on my bed. I picked up an envelope from the bedside table. I read the postmark on the envelope. It was November 29th and was familiar to me. Then I opened the card within the envelope and the signature on the card was "Geneva". I knew immediately who I was and who my family was and it was so good to be alive.

The day before Cliff had been informed by my doctor that he was referring me to the state mental hospital for the insane. He diagnosed me as a hopeless case.

There were no words to describe the broken hearted Cliff as he made his way to the sanitarium to see me for what he thought would be the last time.

When he arrived at my room I smiled and said, "Hello Cliff it's good to see you." We talked and it was apparent that my memory had returned. The result was that the doctor released me and I was allowed to go home with Cliff instead of going to the state mental institution.

All the time I spent in the sanitarium, Tommy had been cared for by my neighbor Mrs. Beasley. She had no children of her own. It was not sure where we would go. The home on the Pigeon Roost Road was being sold and it was such a short notice.

My parents did not want us when we showed up. Cliff went to work and Tommy and I stayed overnight. It was New Years Eve and fireworks were all around the house. I became excited and my emotions ran rapid. I had no idea that it was just fireworks. Already I had sensed the unwelcome attitude of my mother and felt abandoned. When Cliff returned from work the next morning I was a basket case all over again.

Cliff was fortunate to be able to have me admitted to the psychiatric ward of the University of Tennessee Medical Clinic at Knoxville. It was now solely up to me how long I would be taking the new treatment.

In the meantime, Cliff had to find a home for Tommy our seven year old son. My parents refused to care for him. Cliff's sister took him on a trial basis. This worked for a short time.

The best way to describe my illness was to say that some malady had entered my body and destroyed my memory. My physical body was not affected except that I was about 25 pounds underweight.

Time passed and medical aid along with mental rest plus a change of environment aided in my recovery.

My memory since that period of my life has been completely restored. To this day I am able to remember phone numbers, house numbers and all the instances in my life that made an impression. If I speak of some of these memories I receive looks of disapproval and disbelief. Some have said that I have a photographic mind. Even today you may not deem it possible for anyone to have such a memory. It has certainly been an advantage to me to be able to write books with little or no bibliography.

Howard and Tommy

Ready for School

chapter eight

Things Happen

The cause of my strange illness could have been due to the mental strain. My mother shared her good fortune with me over the phone but never any of her material possessions or motherly advice and girl talk. Another thing was the lack of true love in our marriage. I just felt trapped in a situation with no hope of escape. It was true that I was depressed and that it had overwhelmed my sense of reality.

The psychiatrist diagnosed me as a schizophrenic, a person having a mental disorder characterized by indifference, withdrawal, hallucinations, often with impaired intelligence. This diagnosis was a stigma that followed me for years after my illness. My own father wrote to his relatives out of town that I was a mental case. At the time I could not understand that some people put a stamp on you and others understand. I could understand my mother holding onto that belief but my father was a college graduate. I never tried to discuss it with him. One thing the Medical University had right in their diagnosis was that fear had triggered my illness. We found knives in the driver's seat of the truck after my husband drove it home. The dog was poisoned. There was also the scare of the poisonous snakes. The fear may have been caused by mysterious things that happened to us.

While I was a patient of the University of Knoxville at Memphis I was given various treatments and finally the doctor settled on insulin shots. I was one of four patients to take this treatment at this particular time. All four of us were put to sleep by the injection of insulin. Almost instantly we were in a coma. We remained in this coma for a period of time and sometime around lunch time we were awakened from the coma by orange juice. At one time I remember the orange juice being poured down my throat by a tube through my nose.

When all four patients were revived we would be seated at a table loaded with all sorts of breakfast food. The other three patients were obese but on the contrary I was a skeleton so to speak. In the course of two months I had gained twenty five pounds.

My memory at this time had improved enough that I could remember my home phone number and address. My doctor met me in the hallway and asked me for my address. I gave him the right information. He responded by allowing me to go to my home on weekends.

Cliff's sister failed to keep Tommy. She placed him in a Baptist Children's Home. When I was recovered enough to come home on weekends but it was doubtful if I would ever be able to take care of Tommy. I was allowed to go to see Tommy at the home. The head of the home, Dr. Webster, called our son on the loud speaker to come to the office. When Tommy arrived, all out of breath, he exclaimed that he expected a spanking. Nice home, I thought, for my son, Tommy.

The attendant showed us around the place and I saw one large barrel full of socks for all the kids. We saw the room and the bed where Tommy slept. It was all made up nicely. I turned back the covers and saw that it was all wet. Tommy had a habit of wetting the bed sometime. Was he sleeping in a wet bed and no one cared? Each of the children had a chore to do besides making their own bed. How much longer, I thought would it take to rescue Tommy from the home. I never knew if my sister in law ever realized what an impact it had been for a seven year old to be deprived of his home and thrown to the mercy of strangers.

The house on the Pigeon Roost Road had been sold and a house in the city of Memphis on Tutwiler Street was where I came to live. Cliff had bought another home for us.

As time passed I regained the skills to cook, sew and the ability to care for Tommy. He could not return home with us until his school term was over. He failed the second grade.

It took a lot of love, care and concern to prove to Tommy that it was all over now. We had been separated by a cruel fate and now we could be happy to be together once more.

Cliff got boxing gloves and had all the little boys in the neighborhood come over and learn the art of boxing. We had one of the first TV's that came out and there was a greasy dirty spot around the TV where all the little boys sat on the floor. Tommy was adjusting to his new life. There was still a little problem of the older boys trying to show their authority over the younger ones. Cliff taught Tommy how to defend himself. I watched from my window when an older boy kicked dirt on Tommy. He got up and chased that kid across the street to his house and caught him by the shirt tail and pulled the shirt over the kids head and gave him a good spanking. I never mentioned it to Tommy that I had seen this act from my window. The kid as far as I know never kicked any more dirt on Tommy.

chapter nine

New Home in Memphis

Cliff had traded our equity in the house on the Pigeon Roost Road for a house in the city. Tommy was allowed to come to live with Cliff and I when the school semester ended. I was considered well enough to take the responsibility of my son.

I had counted the days until my son would be out of that dreadful children's home. He had failed the second grade and would naturally have to repeat that the following year. The good part was that he would have his parents once more.

The home in the city was a lot different from the one on the Pigeon Roost Road. We could ride busses to work instead of sharing a ride. I could go shopping by riding the bus instead of driving five miles to the edge of town to catch a bus and ride a bus to finally reach the stores to shop. We did without a car temporarily. Tommy could run errands to the grocery for me. Living in the city did have its advantages. Cliff was still working nights and was unable to arise at an early hour to attend church on Sunday. Tommy and I walked to church.

Tommy learned in Sunday school that his body was a temple of God. He was of course taught not to abuse his body. That meant no smoking or drinking. This did not mean that Tommy was by any means a saint. He could have taken to gambling but for some reason he leaned toward his passion for electronics.

Tommy, at nine years old, walked down the long aisle to give his life to Jesus. He had no coaching for this decision. I was surprised and followed him to give my own life to the same Jesus. We were baptized at the same time in a Baptist Church in Memphis.

As we continued our Sunday school activities, my neighbor and long time friend asked me if she could go to my church and take her young sons. I was delighted to have Polly and her sons to go with me. The first Sunday we left the very young sons in the nursery. One of them screamed bloody murder. But Polly walked on toward the Sunday school class with me. A week went by and we again went to take the sons to the nursery. There was no sound of disapproval from Polly's son. We looked at each other and smiled. Many years later I was informed by a friend that Polly had moved to California and the sons were teenagers. They were still in church and Sunday school.

Tommy and his white rabbit

chapter ten

Life in the City

One day after we were living in the big city Tommy came home from the grocery store with Mike his new friend. I noticed that he was holding a package of Dentyne gum.

I knew he was not a gum chewer so I asked where he got the gum. He did not have an answer so I asked if he swiped the gum. Yes he confessed and Mike took a bar of candy. Well I said I am so very glad that a policeman did not see you do that because you and Mike could be arrested for stealing. Tommy to my knowledge did not steal again. It was a different story for Mike because later it was learned that he went to prison at age twenty one for stealing a car.

Alice my best friend and I talked a lot about our lives. We were bored as housewives. We decided that our husbands were out in the working world and exposed to attractive women. When they came home and saw us in hair curlers and no makeup it was a threat to our marriage. So we should brush up on our skills and go to work. We did start to night school and Cliff said OK but you have to make a decent salary.

Well OK I thought so I managed to get a secretary job with a defense plant. The pay was acceptable. My friend never went to work. I was fortunate to get Cleo to do my housework and ride herd on Tommy. I worked a couple of years and Cleo was a maid sent from heaven. There were no permanent pressed clothes back at that time and she ironed all of my handmade cotton dresses. She always found my costume jewelry and put it in place on my vanity. If cotton picking season came then Cleo took to the fields. We had to do for ourselves during these times. All the time that Cleo was there my house was spotless.

Tommy learned to ride his bike. Soon after this he developed a knot in his lower right side. The doctor said it was a hernia and immediate surgery was needed. So Tommy had the surgery and everything went well. When he was returned to his room (there was no recovery room back in the forties) and he remained in a semi-conscious state. His face was flushed and his hands were ice cold and actually clammy. I panicked and went in search of the nurse. There were no nurses at the station so I ran down the long hall until I could find someone to help. When I did locate an attendant the whole crew came running to Tommy's room. His blood pressure had dropped and the drug that had been used to put him to sleep for the surgery was blocking his recovery. They elevated the foot of his bed and gave him oxygen and after what seemed an eternity he opened his eyes. What a scare. What a close call. In those days a patient was given ether or gas to prepare the patient for the surgery. My advice to any mother is to stay with your child in the hospital during this critical time. Tommy did recover from the surgery and was home before we knew it.

My work as a secretary for a few years provided me with enough experience to apply for a government position. My first job happened to be in the procurement office where prime contracts were initiated for the world. All of our work had to be proof read and accuracy was required. The salary was above average and promotions were easy to attain. I only worked one year when Cliff was fired from his job. He had been employed by the Memphis Street Railway Company about twelve years. He was unable to connect with another job that was comparable to his former position. Naturally he became restless and one day I came home from work and the car was gone. So was Cliff. Just like that. No note and no sign except that his clothes were missing.

Little did I know where or why he had left home. Problems never ceased. A window pane was broken out and Tommy fixed it. Then the roof leaked and one of Cliff's friends fixed that for a fee.

After about six weeks Cliff was back to get Tommy and me to return to California with him. He had a two bit job at a very small town with the Southern Pacific Railroad Company. Well his clothes were stained by the water in this town so I could not see any future in rushing to live there. I refused to follow Cliff on this venture.

Cliff was all aglow about the beauty and prosperity in California. We had once contemplated going to California to live ten years prior to this time. I chose to keep on with my job. So Cliff went to work as a pie salesman. That failed to be profitable so he switched to selling family reference bibles. He teamed up with another man and they were doing quite well. They travelled together and made shows and fairs and sold all kinds of bibles. Also they could sell bible story books. They could sell anywhere in the country and that was a plus.

chapter eleven

Cleo My Angel Maid

I gave a Bunko Party while Cleo was employed as a maid. She normally cleaned house on Wednesday and did the ironing on Tuesday. My party was set for Tuesday evening at 7 PM. I asked Cleo to switch days and to clean on Tuesday.

I came home from work on Tuesday and to my unsuspecting surprise the house was a holy mess. There were beautifully ironed clothes staring me in the face. Cleo had forgotten.

Well what do you do in a crisis but get to work to first hang up the clothes, get the house in order and put the ice cream in the refrigerator. I had two hours to do a days work to get ready to play hostess.

The weather certainly did not cooperate for it suddenly turned cool and the heat was turned off. When the guest began to arrive I was ready to go straight up. Cliff returned home from a fishing trip and had caught fish. What in the blessed world could possibly happen next?

I had skipped my dinner and the smelly fish made me nauseated. I asked Cliff to clean his fish on the back porch and not to be seen in the house for a bit. At least until the party was over. OK he responded.

When it came time to serve the ice cream and cake one of my guest had a chill. My heavens could anything else happen on this fateful night?

Finally they all left and everything would you believe returned to normal. The result however, was that I resigned from the Bunko Club.

Tommy in Mobile Bay

Tennessee Memories

Electrical storms were common in Memphis and one fateful night we had a bad one. As a rule I slept through these storms and this night I did sleep through it. The next morning we awoke and found a large tree that was growing in our yard had been struck by lightning and laid across the yard next door to us. The only damage was to knock out a section of our fence.

When Tommy was about ten years old he and I went to the Ringling Brothers Circus while Cliff was at work. It was a giant affair and held in the auditorium which covered a city block.

We started home and decided to go by Cliff's place of employment. As we approached the entrance we spotted our car parked outside the door. Cliff needed the car because he had no transportation when he got off work at 2:30 AM.

I noticed two teenage girls sitting inside the car. I walked over to the car and asked if they were waiting for someone? They both nodded and one girl said we are waiting for Broadway. Well OK I thought I will just go inside and see him. When Cliff had a minute to talk I asked who the girls were in our car? He did not answer me but just shot out the door like a bullet. There was never an explanation about who the girls were. On second look they both appeared to be over sixteen.

Tommy and I came home on the city bus and I regret not taking the car. The subject never came up again and it did nothing for our marital bliss.

If your mate comes home late from work and disappears on his days off work what do you do? What do you think? I had nowhere to go and Tommy was not old enough to work. I knew I could not make it alone. I kept silent about it all.

During the next few years we had our ups and downs as we lived there in the city of Memphis. Cliff's teeth went bad and he needed dentures. His dentist extracted 14 teeth and inserted a new set of dentures. Cliff was in agony.

A Russian immigrant friend came by the house. He mixed a loaded cocktail for Cliff and shortly Cliff passed out. He did not wake up until the next morning.

Cliff could have died from the overdose of Novocain and alcohol but by the grace of God he lived.

We seemed to be protected from a lot of bad situations. One day while I was on sick leave and Tommy was at home. He was about ten years old at the time and I had taken a sleeping pill. Tommy was playing around the house and I was somewhat groggy. Suddenly he called me. I arose from my bed and entered the room where I saw my son holding two wires in his hands that were connected to an electronic device that was given to him and plugged into the wall outlet. He apparently could not let go of the electric wires. I quickly unplugged the light cord from the wall socket and Tommy was released.

A miracle had just taken place for my son, Tommy had AC current going through his body and could not move. It scared him enough to keep him away from his adventure in a world that he knew little about. That world was electricity and he learned that it was dangerous.

Tommy at an early age in life returned to the public library to learn all he could about electricity. Today he is well versed on this subject and so am I.

There were many fun times in Memphis as Tommy grew up. Like the backyard barbecues that we attended at Cliff's mother's house. These times were always so much fun because Cliff's sisters acted like they were on a New York stage and they sang the old songs that went with their acts. All the Memphis Blues Songs that W.C. Handy wrote. Basin Street Blues was the one about New Orleans and it was of course the favorite. It was like they had flipped their lids when they would shout Mama look what she did to me. I loved them when they were happy and having fun with each other.

The first night I met Cliff he took me to his house and two of his sisters were there. They ran to the attic to recover some of the 1920 coats, scarfs and hats to wear when they rode in Cliff's open top car. The car name was Lou Ella.

We stopped at a roadside café and one sister ordered a hot dog with a lot of mustard. She kept squeezing the hot dog in and out of the bun and looking like Harpo Marx. They were just teasing their brother because he had a new girl friend. Anything for a laugh, you had to have a sense of humor just to tolerate them. Mom Broadway just laughed at all of the crazy behavior.

Cliff's car was a model A Ford roadster and no top, but had a rumble seat. There were three seated in the rumble seat. Cliff's sister, another sister Louise and a friend Cookie, all rode in the rumble seat. They wanted to observe their brother with his new girl friend. The windshield was broken on the passenger side so the passenger had to sit close to the driver. His family knew this. So I sat close to the driver while they watched.

Cliff's family was taught to stick together no matter what happened to them. It had been them against the world since their father had died of TB in the thirties. They stuck together and I was an outsider. Cliff and I continued the same tradition after we were married. If Cliff was in trouble I was right there by his side to fight the world. The same with me if I had anything to go wrong it was surely Cliff's problem and Cliff was there to fight with me. As Tommy came into our family he was just as much a part of the same tradition. We banded together as a family.

Cliff, our Moms and me

Cliff's Mom

chapter twelve

Leaving Tennessee

We decided after a lot of discussion to sell out and head for the great state of California. The first step was to sell our home and we took a second mortgage to be paid monthly to insure an income until we were settled in our new living space. We bought a house trailer and a better car so that Cliff could sell the family bibles along the way to California. School was out for the summer so we did not hurry to reach our destination.

We picked San Bernardino as a possible place to look for employment at Norton Air Force Base. Norton did not turn out as we had anticipated. The salaries were less than private employment.

We had been on the road about thirty days. Our first stop had been Oklahoma City. We parked in a trailer park and drove to the publishing company by car. We purchased a supply of bibles at Wichita, Kansas. Then we continued with the trailer to Albuquerque, New Mexico. Cliff's older sister lived there. We stayed there in a trailer park about two weeks. Cliff's sister, Kathryn treated us to our first Mexican food at a restaurant in Old Town.

Cliff drove to Grant, New Mexico where he sold about five hundred dollars worth of bibles. There were no banks and the people had cash money to spend. Grant was a uranium boom town in the fifties. Uranium was discovered there and the government took over that project. Businesses sprang up everywhere. Cafes, beauty shops, service stations, grocery stores and liquor stores were numerous.

Cliff was having a salesman dream. He sold out the supply of bibles that we had bought in Wichita. The load in the trailer was lightened somewhat.

In August Indian Celebrations were held each year. Gallup was the Indian Capital of the country. Tommy was busy on his portable radio listening to everything that was going on in Gallup and all parts of New Mexico.

The weather during the time we were in New Mexico was very unusual. It rained in one spot while a few feet away the ground would be dry. The Rio Grande River runs through Albuquerque. We had stayed in Albuquerque as long as we could stay so it was time to move on. We told Cliff's sister goodbye and headed for the state of California.

chapter thirteen

Tommy's Birth

I began to remember back before Tommy was born. I was going to see my doctor for my checkup when I was about eight months in my pregnancy. I was riding on an ancient street car that ran on rails like a train. All at once there was a terrible jolt and it knocked my hat off. We had been hit from behind by another street car. The rear of the street car was demolished. All around me the people were groaning and moaning and everyone seemed confused by what had just happened. The motorman came to me with a pad and pen to get my claim for injuries. I was feeling no pain but he took my name anyway. When all had signed up for claims we were transferred to another street car.

I was not injured apparently and Tommy was born August 9, 1943 at the Methodist Hospital in Memphis, Tennessee. The day I went to the hospital I was on a bus and fell into my seat. My back began to hurt and I said nothing until we got home. When I told Cliff I had back pain he rushed me to the hospital. They put me in a bed and I lay there for twenty seven hours. At last my doctor came and they took me to the operating room and put me to sleep. When I awoke it was all over. They put me in a room and Cliff said it was a boy.

When morning came they brought me Tommy. He just slept and did not nurse for three days. I was weak and I lay on my side and scooted Tommy close to my heart and loved him.

Months later I received a check in the mail for $600.00 and Cliff and I deposited it in the bank. Tommy was a small baby then and I thought now we have a nest egg. Cliff worked for the street car company and a Mr. Fischer had approved the money we had received.

I trusted Cliff and thought he felt the same as I did about the money we had in the bank. I was mistaken. Later I checked the balance of the account and to my great surprise we had only $13.00 left.

Cliff had yielded to his mania for gambling and helped himself to our money. Of course he was sorry because he had not won when he bet our money. He never replaced the money but kept on gambling. He was good at heart and always supported Tommy and me. I guess that's life and we can't be perfect.

We named Tommy after Cliff's friend in the US Navy and Tommy's middle name was Graves after Cliff. The friend was proud to have a namesake and bought a china cat in China and sent it to us. I still have the cat and had to glue it back together when it was broken in about a dozen pieces.

chapter fourteen

Cliff's Early Life

When Cliff was eleven his father died and he was one of eight kids. They all took to the street to support their Mom. One day Cliff was playing ball in the street with other boys. He hit a baseball and broke out a stained glass window in a beautiful old Episcopal Cathedral and the Dean in charge came out to see what the boys were up to. He took them inside and promptly converted them.

The Dean converted them all to Jesus Christ of Nazareth. He then committed them to church services. They all became altar boys and Cliff was the leader or the one altar boy to serve the bishop the wine when he was present.

Cliff became very close to the pastor. Soon after, the pastor began a forty day fast, which began on Ash Wednesday in February until Easter Sunday. Cliff was his right hand man. The pastor's family deserted him because of all the publicity.

The newspaper did articles and pictures of the fast every week. The pictures in the paper showed the pastor losing weight and at the last days of the fast he appeared to be a skeleton. He had been fasting on cashew nuts and orange juice. He dropped from about 200 pounds to around 100 pounds in the forty days. When Easter Sunday came he was still alive.

Cliff's name was never mentioned in the paper. About ten years later I became the wife of Cliff. He related the whole story to me of the fast. We met with the pastor and he blessed our marriage. Later when Tommy was born he was baptized in the church by the Dean.

Pastor Dean Noe fell dead on his church grounds when Tommy was about fourteen years of age. I was working for the Sun Company newspaper and just happened to set the obituary for the linotype machine. I was made aware of the death of the pastor. I was in California and the pastor was in Tennessee.

Cliff's life was spent working to support his widowed mother and going to school. He managed to graduate from high school. He was trained to follow the pastor and to go to a seminary to be an Episcopal priest but he did not go that way because of his family needs. I have his prayer book which has been updated since he used it in services.

Cliff sewed his wild oats and became the prodigal son. He enlisted in the US Army and spent a year and was medically discharged when he had a posterior dislocated right shoulder. The army did not want him if he could not fire a rifle. In 1942 he was out of the service and married to me.

So for the duration of the war Cliff had a medical discharge from the US Army. He had all the veteran benefits. He replaced a man who had been drafted into the military service.

Tommy's Mother   Tommy's Father

chapter fifteen

California Bound

We arrived in California, tired, weary and worn from all our travels. We had been on the road for thirty days selling bibles. September was around the corner and school would be starting soon. Tommy was eager to start junior high school. We managed to find a trailer park close to Arrowhead Junior High School.

Our neighbor in the park worked for the Santa Fe Railroad. He notified Cliff that a job was open for a heavy equipment operator. Cliff was inexperienced but was hired for the job anyway. It was a good thing because the bibles were not in demand in our part of the state. We needed the income as the second mortgage payment check was not enough to live on.

Later on I got work at the local newspaper but that first year in California was a pip. We were penalized by the state both for our car and trailer for expired licenses. We were ignorant of the California laws. Everything did work out for us because Cliff made overtime pay enough to pay those extra expenses and to see us through these tough times.

We learned to live a life of independence away from our relatives in Memphis. The Pigeon Roost Road had been an education for us but this new adventure in California was a whole new ball game. We became pioneers living in the other part of the country.

Cliff always said to me if anything ever happens to me I know you will survive. "You are in this world but not of this world."

Cliff's job resulted in one of those away from home deals so after a year I had begun work at the newspaper in town and working a three to eleven shift so that left Tommy pretty much on his own. He was thirteen years old by that time and could be trusted to do for himself and stay out of trouble. Living in a trailer park was not as bad as in a house. At least he had friends close by.

Since Cliff was gone for months at a time and our lives were like me living as a single parent and I tried to make the best of the situation. There were times when I had to deal with overbearing tough individuals.

Once there was a fight between Tommy and a neighborhood boy. I had to investigate why the kid had punched Tommy in the temple. I came face to face with the kid's mother and she had red hair and was a bartender in a local bar. She seemed to support her son for jumping on my son in their yard for his acts. The whole thing was so uncalled for and I had to tell this woman she could in the future keep her son away from us if she cared about his safety. I never had any more trouble with them. I did see them again and they crossed the street to keep from meeting me face to face again.

If Cliff had been there he would have reacted in a much different way I am sure. So when Cliff got back home we moved to another trailer park across town. I met some nice people that were caring and compassionate.

My father's background helped me to know and understand strangers as he was a graduate of Vanderbilt University in Nashville,

Tennessee. Some of the ones I met could only talk on one subject which was the key to the story of their lives. Other people that I met were down and out and if you helped them they would be your friend for life but still be always ready for another favor from you.

Cliff told me once that if anything happened to him that he was certain that I could support myself and Tommy. Furthermore he said "I hope it never comes to this but if you ever have to defend yourself you know a few dirty tricks to play so remember one thing that the bigger they come the harder they fall."

We could never depend on Cliff's pay checks because he had a habit of betting a whole check and then to cover his loss of the money he would either borrow the money or mortgaging the furniture to replace it. We just did not try to have a bank account and lived pay day to pay day. The money was always there when Cliff felt lucky. Cliff would even write a counter check on our checking account. If I was out of town and needed money I was reluctant to write a check without knowing the current balance of our account. My life was very insecure.

While Cliff was working in Arizona, one of the railroad employees knocked on my door late at night. He said that Cliff had been involved in a bad accident. I asked him through the locked door about his knowledge of the accident.

His information did not make sense. He left and I went back to bed and tried to go to sleep. The thought of maybe it did happen was very annoying to me. The next morning I called the Santa Fe office in San Bernardino and inquired about the accident. There was no such accident. My husband's superior said to, "Lock your door"

Cliff was a born comedian and always had some silly comical answer when he was confronted by people. He came home time and again to tell me of how his expressions were sending the men he worked with into gales of laughter. For example, if he said he wanted a piece of pie it was not what he said but the way he said it. They would come back at him and to get him to repeat it would say what did you say? He would then tell them that he could not HEP it. They would then fall over in gales of laughter. Cliff could not change as he was just dripping with a real southern accent.

The only train that ran to Richmond was the Chief which was a very nice train. On one trip I was seated in a compartment with a bed and meals were brought to me so I could stay until I reached my destination. It was so nice to feel like a VIP for a short time. Tommy would be at the train station to meet me.

Cliff and I made a trip to see Tommy on his twenty first birthday while he was working at Richmond. We went to dinner at Joe DiMaggio's Restaurant at Fishermen's Wharf and it was a swanky place. The glasses on the tables were all souvenirs because they had Joe and his bat printed on them. I wanted to steal one and I told Tommy to put it in his camera case. He turned his head and looked all around then picked up the glass. Nobody ever said anything so maybe they expected you to take them.

I took another trip to see Tommy and that was a laugh just getting on the train. I took a portable sewing machine in a case that appeared to be a part of my luggage.

The porter rushed to pick up my luggage and put it on the train. It must have weighed a ton and I watched the porters face as he picked up the luggage. I do not remember how I got it to the station platform in the first place unless my husband had brought it. At any rate to get it on the train required a nice tip for the porter.

There was still another trip to Richmond that I remember and that was a very nice memory. It was a night trip and the train stopped in the Tehachapi Mountains to let another train pass. I was seated in the lounge car and the conductor of the train came to me and invited me to step outside the last car. He wanted me to see the beautiful sight of the pine trees that were covered with snow and bending over the train and the track. They were so close you could touch them. I shall never forget the natural beauty of that glorious experience.

chapter sixteen

Tommy in Junior High School

When Tommy began in Arrowhead Junior High School he could walk to school. He liked the school in California because it was much different from the schools in Tennessee. He worked for the school by washing the pots and pans for credits in school. He was active in sports and obtained a sweater with a big "A" on it.

They had an exhibit and Tommy entered his project. It was actually something that had not been invented. It was a home made radio that was turned on automatically by a device that sensed the presence of a person's body or hand. This was similar to the way doors are opened today when you approach the door. He only got third prize. The first prize went to the son of one of the teachers on staff.

Tommy's exhibit was entered in the San Bernardino County Science Fair Exhibit and captured first prize. He got a red ribbon instead of a blue one for runner up. His name was in the newspaper.

We moved across town and Tommy changed schools. He was into sports and was a broad jumper. He held the record for his school which was Highland Junior High School.

All went well until Tommy graduated from junior high and started high school. That was a different situation. There were two high schools in San Bernardino and Pacific High was the desired school.

Tommy attended Pacific High School until his sophomore year. After Cliff and I separated Tommy and I moved to Memphis, Tennessee. He was enrolled in Central High School. Central was the elite school in the city of Memphis. Mr. Branyan was his electronics teacher. Tommy enrolled in a special class to obtain a Federal Communication First Class Radio Telephone License.

When Tommy finished school a job at a Communications Repair Shop was available. So he took the job and began his first job.

chapter seventeen

New Job

Tommy wanted to be in California. He called his father at the Santa Fe Railroad Company for help. Cliff went to the Radio Shop of the Santa Fe and asked for Tommy to work. Since Tommy had the proper credentials he was hired. So Tommy came to California. After he started to work he was bumped to a job in Los Angeles. He worked a couple of weeks and was bumped to Winslow, Arizona. It was in the dead of winter and in the middle of nowhere. The bids came up and Tommy bid on Richmond, California.

When Tommy worked for the Santa Fe, in Richmond, he always worked with Mr. Wilson, who had been there forever. One of the duties was to maintain the radar equipment on the tug boats in the bay area. Tommy had a radar endorsement on his FCC license, so he was well qualified to work there. Mr. Wilson was a good friend. They got along famously and when Mr. Wilson stuffed an old cigar into his pipe and smoked it the smell was unbearable to some, but Tommy just rolled down the truck window and let in some fresh air.

When he was twenty one years of age Uncle Sam claimed him in the draft. Tommy rushed to the Air Force Recruiting Station and enlisted in the United States Air Force for four years.

Tommy completed his boot camp training in Lackland Air Force Base, Texas. The other recruits were sent to tech schools while Tommy was already licensed in radio communication. He was ordered to Langley Field, Newport News, Virginia. Approximately a year later Tommy was ordered to Korea. I breathed a sigh of relief when I received this bit of news. It was expected that he would end up in Vietnam. After thirteen months in Korea Tommy came marching home! We met him at LAX.

We enjoyed Tommy's leave from the service and he was ordered to Altus, Oklahoma at Altus Air Force Base. About six months later he received a six month early out. He was discharged from the United States Air Force.

Tommy's job with the Santa Fe Railroad was waiting for him when he was released from the Air Force. There was no one qualified to maintain the tug boat radar except Tommy and Mr. Wilson.

At first, Tommy ate his meals in a neighborhood restaurant and the owner accepted payments on a weekly basis.

One bad experience for Tommy was an impacted wisdom tooth and surgery was performed. He bled for three days but never missed a day at work. Maybe he was afraid of losing his job if he did not show up for work.

Later that year my father passed away after a short bout with cancer. I was in Memphis with my parents. Tommy and Cliff were notified and came for the funeral.

Back in Richmond, Tommy often visited a friend, who also worked for the railroad. He was the father of four children. Tommy had a common interest of Ham radio. So he would enjoy the hobby with his friend.

Tommy later moved into a furnished house. He could then invite friends over to watch TV and eat catered food. Darrel, a friend from Junior High in San Bernardino, came to spend about four days. He had been one of Tommy's Ham Radio friends.

chapter eighteen

Air Force Bound

It was about February 1964 that Tommy got an invitation from Uncle Sam to be enlisted in the military service. He rapidly enlisted in the Air Force for a four year period. That meant that Tommy had to move out of the rented house and I had to help him. How in the world I thought as I entered his house could anyone restore it to what it was when he had rented it. Oh, I was beside myself when I looked around the jumbled mess in every room. I almost walked back out the door or sat down hopelessly in a chair. But no it had to be done. There was a way and we did manage to straighten out that holy mess.

All of the pictures were scattered throughout the apartment. All of the furniture had to be restored, and polished. All of the shades were off the lamps and shades on the windows were not being used. The refrigerator had never been defrosted while Tommy lived there and ice was four inches thick on the freezing unit. The gas cook stove was cleaned even though Tommy had only used it to heat water. The floors were dirty and the carpets were stained. All of the curtains were pushed back to let in more light. An ironing board was being used as an extra table and it was loaded with nuts, bolts and screws. It took a solid week to restore it all. We invited the owner to inspect her property before Tommy moved out.

Sometimes you cannot win. That lady walked right over to the gas cook stove and opened a tray under the burners and found dirt. For that reason she denied Tommy the rent deposit.

The following week Tommy left to go to boot camp at Lackland Field, Texas. He was so versed in communication that after his boot camp he was assigned to on the job instead of being trained for his future work in the service.

His new assignment was Langley Field AFB in Newport News, Virginia. That is the strategic air base that guards the White House and Washington, DC. This was in the sixties and Viet Nam was the hot spot.

chapter nineteen

Uncle Bill

I shall never forget Uncle Bill's visit to see us in Memphis when Tommy was about six years old. It was during the time that we lived on the Pigeon Roost Road.

It was such a pleasure for me to know my uncle for the very first time. He was such a unique person and unlike anyone. He was my mother's brother but they were not alike in any way.

He had been adopted at an early age by a well to do farmer in Texas. He was separated from my mother and his family. After his graduation from high school he joined the Seabees during World War 1. After his discharge he made his home in Southern California.

He was so full of stories and told us about being in Hawaii when Pearl Harbor was bombed. It was his duty as a telegrapher to notify the commanding officer of the brutal attack by the Japanese.

Of all places, Uncle Bill chose Hollywood. He married a potential starlet and they became the parents of a son. They left Hollywood and moved up the coast to central California.

Two daughters were born after about ten years. Uncle Bill was a telegrapher and was employed by the Southern Pacific Railroad. When the girls were small he lost his wife. No one on earth could take the place of his beautiful wife. Uncle Bill was a deep lover. A housekeeper was found who had a son and a daughter and she took good care of his girls and kept his house neat and clean. She happened to be the Post Mistress in the small town where they lived. Uncle Bill married this wonderful lady and she passed away in 1958.

Later Uncle Bill sought the companionship of his siblings. All his life he had been separated from them. There were brothers in Texas and his sister in Memphis.

My parents were temporarily living with me at the time on the Pigeon Roost Road. He found us and I do not know how he did that.

Uncle Bill's adopted family lived on a good farm and he knew a lot about farming. Of course that was what we needed to know.

My mother, Julia was so happy to once again be with her favorite brother. When he left he gave us his address and mother kept in touch with him. When vacation came, my parents made their first trip to California to see Uncle Bill and his family. One girl was married and had three daughters. The other daughter was on an assignment job in Germany. She worked for Stanford University and was a divorcee. In spite of his being a widower he lived to be 93 years old. He passed away in 1985 in Greenfield, California.

chapter twenty

Cancer Struck

Six years after we moved to Barstow we were informed that Cliff had cancer. He was admitted to the Santa Fe Hospital for tests. No diagnosis for certain so we saw a doctor in San Bernardino and found it to be cancer of the pancreas. Cliff was doomed to go back to the Santa Fe Hospital to be covered by insurance.

I drove to the Santa Fe Hospital in Los Angeles and Cliff had surgery that day. When I arrived I was told that his liver had been bypassed from the pancreas and that would give him another seven months to live and also clear up the yellow jaundice he had. I returned to my car parked on the street to find a citation for illegal parking for that particular day. Troubles never cease.

Cliff spent seven months in the hospital and passed away. He was finally out of pain. It was 1972 and we were fortunate to have had twenty nine years of marriage. He was only fifty four and had lived life to the fullest. Guess I had done the same and still had life to live and I was just forty nine. My best friend drove me to the hospital to make the arrangements for his burial.

It wasn't easy to live alone and pay for a car and a thirty year mortgage. I cut out all the unnecessary expenses like the newspaper and TV and conserved on lights, gas and water. I made few trips to the grocery store. My friends helped me some. If I really needed something I could call on the Masonic Lodge. There were a few times when I needed maintenance that I could not afford. Of course I did not remain in this situation for very long.

I had not worked in the past ten years and it was apparent that I would have no income from Cliff's work. There was some insurance money but try and live on that. I would be broke and then what?

To get employment was the only answer. I found two bit jobs but could not live on those salaries. After about six months I was working in a Justice Court on a livable salary. Tommy was living in Richmond, California and working for the Santa Fe. I dared not to call on him for any financial help.

I succeeded in obtaining a position with the County Civil Service and the Court was what I had the opportunity to get. I worked for a Justice Court in Yermo, California and it was merged with the Justice Court in Barstow. The end result was a municipal court. I remained with this job until I resigned in 1975.

chapter twenty-one

Cliff was buried

After the funeral for Tommy's father, Cliff, I returned to my job at the Justice Court and tried to get on with my life. It was the hardest thing for me to do. I really did not have any close friends and relatives were not in California. I just lived alone except for the time that Tommy stayed in my town.

I began to think about the fact that I had no grandchildren. Tommy was past thirty and not even engaged. I prayed that he would find the right woman and settle down. That would be my only hope to be a grandmother. It would be so nice at this stage of my life to cradle a baby in my arms. My daily prayers were that some day and somehow that this would happen.

Three and a half years passed and I was still a frustrated grandmother. I was fifty three and going through the menopause when I was told I had to have a hysterectomy. The loss of blood had caused me to have anemia most of the time. I did manage to keep working and just six months later everything changed.

I met Sterling Wood, who was the father of my neighbor across the street. I had met him before and we became good friends. We were married in 1975 and we traveled on short trips in California. Sterling met my son Tommy and he said he believed that a marriage would be in the making. My hopes were high for Tommy.

We visited Sterling's daughter, Susan across the street and she told us that she was to have a baby the following year. She said that it was for me to be grandma. Susan had lost her mother and she needed a mom so that was up to me. Sterling had two daughters Susan and Marny. I had one son so the kids appreciated the new family we had. I just had to send up a prayer for small favors.

Sure enough Susan's baby arrived and was my granddaughter from the start. She was named Stacie Elizabeth and wore my gift of a little yellow dress home from the hospital.

I was so gratified to cradle little Stacie in my arms, I loved her and hoped that she would love me back. I saw her get her first bath and her first time to go outside the house. We saw that she was dressed in her tiny pinafores and always a ribbon in her hair, really what little hair she had. She did get hair and then it was most of the time in a pony tail.

It was only natural that Stacie would find her way across the street to my house. She had a small piece of luggage and would put her gown, toothbrush and shoes in the case and make her way across the street to my house. She spent the night quite a bit and if I told her to go back home if she could not drink her milk she drank it whether she liked it or not.

Stacie became a cheerleader in elementary school. So I had to make her cheerleader costume. We were just one happy family. I loved sewing for my granddaughter.

When Stacie became a teenager she joined the Masonic Rainbow Assembly in our home town of Barstow. We went shopping for her first formal dress. It was a pink satin dress and good heavens it was the most expensive. I bought the dress and grandpa did not mind at all to pay $150 for the dress.

Lois Heiser, the Mother Advisor of Rainbow, was my friend for many years and she took over Stacie's Rainbow life. My dream of course was for Stacie to go for it. She did and went all the way to the top and became Worthy Advisor.

My granddaughter was surely growing up and was in junior high school. She became a member of the school band. Her hair was long and I had to braid it to fit under the cap she had to wear. She remained in the band for a couple of years. All the while she was doing remarkable jobs in Rainbow. A lot of her assignments were to memorize long passages and to recite all of these.

Stacie went on to the drama class in high school and played many parts in school plays. One very long bit of memory was devoted to the part of narrator for the Christmas play "Scrooge"

After graduation Stacie was torn by the decision of joining the WAVES or going to college. She did neither but moved herself to Phoenix, Arizona. Her father Lefty Grant who was a meat cutter at the Safeway Store backed her as she worked and cleaned house for a friend for her room and board in Phoenix and after two years she returned home.

It was Lefty that introduced Stacie to Kevin. They fell in love and Kevin proposed marriage. It turned out to be a fairy tale marriage. The marriage ended in a divorce after two years. Stacie became a single parent of her two children.

Stacie remarried nine years after the divorce to Kevin. She is happy now. We at the present time await the birth of Little Autumn. Stacie plans to return to college when her daughter is born.

chapter twenty-two

Tommy's Grandparents

All the time Tommy was in the Air Force I corresponded with my parents. I was in California and they were in Memphis, Tennessee.

They were at last living a life of luxury due to the fact that they had a good income from a government job. They could travel mostly to visit my mother's side of the family. They made a couple of trips to California to see me. They also visited my uncle Bill in King City, California.

My mother seemed to take her material possessions for granted. All during the hard times we endured in the great depression, she had referred to Matthew 7:7 which reads "ask and it shall be given thee, seek and ye shall find; knock and it shall be opened unto you."

Now that she was blessed she seemed to forget church. My father actually ran from the preacher when it came to money. The preacher had stood by him all during the great depression.

A few years passed and my poor father had a bad heart attack and was forced to retire. He could no longer afford to travel. He was worried that he could not pay the mortgage before he died.

When I was born my father declared that I was a million dollar baby in a dollar store. He spoiled me rotten and then on his death bed he told me that he had never conquered me. Believe me he tried.

It happened in 1963 my father died of stomach cancer. My mother was in a state of shock and could not arrange the funeral. He was buried in Elmwood Cemetery in his beloved Memphis, Tennessee.

chapter twenty-three

Grandmother's Last Days

Tommy's grandmother spent her last days in California near me. She outlived his grandfather twenty five years. Her life was not spent in vain. Most of her life was taking care of grandfather.

She believed the important things in life were to be tolerant up to a point. When everything went too far she would draw the line and that's it. No more!

Tommy's grandmother was my angel mother. All I am or ever hope to be I owe to her. She had a way of supplying me with good information.

Mother always came up with a solution to our problems. When we needed money she would clean house or iron for somebody. One day while she was out working my father decided to give me a laxative pill. Maybe he thought I needed it. He of course got a leather strap to force me to take that big pill. It was the only laxative in the house at the time. I finally put the pill in my mouth and the sugar coating came off making it very bitter. It was making me sick and I knew I had to somehow spit it out. My father became distracted for a second and I ran for the front door. When I opened the door the porch was a solid sheet of ice. No stopping now so I skated across the porch and landed in a snow pile. I looked back and my father was standing in the doorway. I knew he wasn't going to follow me. So I got up and went to find my angel mother. I found her.

I should be happy that my life was as good as it was. My mother made up for all the unhappy times. She never rebelled against my father but seemed to have a way of sweet talking him to do her way.

Grandmother was "Nana" to Tommy and she was in her glory when she could have him to spend the night at her home. One day she asked if he loved his wrinkled up grandma and Tommy remarked, "I love you but not your wrinkles."

In 1956 Tommy moved with Cliff and me to California. It was devastating for Tommy's grandparents to see him go. Tommy seemed to miss them both.

Years passed and grandfather passed away. After five years of living alone in Memphis Tommy's grandmother came to live in California. She made her home with Cliff and me. Tommy was at the time in the US Air Force.

Grandmother lived another twenty five years and had her own apartment. She participated in many senior activities. She attended church regularly. In her circle of friends she was highly thought of by everyone.

Two years before mother passed away she had dementia and turned against me. She accused me of stealing from her. She called the police and reported me to them. Finally she was taken to a home where she died two years later. I had tried to take care of her and it hurt me that she had to go that way.

chapter twenty-four

A Widow at Forty Nine

It was the year of 1972 when Cliff passed away in the ATSF Hospital in Los Angeles. Tommy had transferred to Barstow, California to be near his father. Each weekend we made the trip to the hospital for about ten months when Cliff died. We buried him in Barstow. Tommy after a few months returned to his job in the Bay Area. He was at the time employed by ATSF.

I was without an income so it was necessary to go to work. I had not worked in ten years and it was hard to get started again in the working force. I took some civil service tests for the government, the county and the state. This was slow going for anyone. It was six months before any positions were available.

I took the first opportunity as a waitress job and I was not experienced. I went through agony with my feet the first week. My tips were scant and it was a big chore to keep going. One of my friends got me a job in a credit bureau and the boss was a tyrant. I worked one month and quit that job. In two weeks one of my efforts paid off. The county called me for a job thirty miles from home. Then another call came through for a job in the local library. I went in for an interview and the man asked me if I would rat on another employee if I saw them doing something wrong. I looked at him and his hair was dirty and he was not a very clean looking individual and something turned me against the hope of a job working there. I responded to his question in the affirmative and left with no regret of not taking that job. My next call came from the San Bernardino County Civil Service. It was at a Justice Court in Yermo, California.

Well this time the future looked brighter the judge of the Justice Court was a kind soul and the office of young women looked OK so I decided that this must be the job for me.

I went to work at the Justice Court without telling the judge that my husband was at the point of death. One month later Cliff died and the news was known to the judge and the office clerks. The sympathy of the whole office went out for me. The judge offered me some time off from work but I refused his offer. I felt that I was on stage in life and the show goes on no matter what happens. Cliff was buried and I only missed one day of work.

The job at the Justice Court was a Godsend and kept me in focus of what I had to do. Some days my eyes filled with tears when no one was looking but I kept on in my daily chores.

After six months passed my son moved away and I felt a big loss in my security. You just don't quit in the middle of the stream so I went to work each day as usual. It is not easy when you live alone. A few years passed and I did survive.

The Justice Court merged with another Justice Court in the area and became a Municipal Court. I was transferred with the office crew to the new court. It meant a raise in pay. I had to get accustomed to working with the new employees. I felt alone and abandoned at times but the knowledge that I had to succeed was important to me. Cliff had told me that I could survive on my own and that was it.

I came home from work one day and I was so depressed. I felt that I could not endure another day of life. I remembered a friend had given me a phone number to call for help. I called and a voice answered from St. Louis, Missouri. He asked what was my reason for the call? Well I had to work for a living and I was not sure of my job or if I could go on with my life.

The kind voice assured me that God would provide for me in a bountiful way for all my needs. I believed what he was saying to me. I went to work the next day and I knew that everything in my life was going to be okay.

All of the insurance money that I had received plus the retirement pay that Cliff had with the Santa Fe was tied up in an investment that even I could not touch.

I cut out all of the extra expenses like the TV, the newspaper and the fun stuff and tried to live within my income. I went to church and the lodge Cliff had belonged to. I knew a lot of people, but few knew what I was experiencing in my personal life except my husband's friends who were sympathetic and I could have had favors from them if I had asked. Also the Masonic Lodge would have been there if I needed them. I belonged to the women's organization at the lodge and was active. They were dependent on my services. This kept me busy at times. I still felt alone most of the time.

One bright spot in my life was the children in my neighborhood and they would come to see me when I was home. It was little Kristine across the street who came over each day. She told me her grandmother had died. So I became her substitute Grandmother. I combed the tangles out of her long hair and she played with her Barbie dolls under my big shade tree. Many times she brought her little friends.

chapter twenty-five

New Father

Kristine had grown to be a teenager and her brother Greg came one day and said that his grandfather would like to meet me. I quickly responded by telling Greg to bring his grandfather over some day. I closed the door and the phone rang.

It was my dinner companion calling to break the engagement so that left me free to rest up from a busy week. Believe me, I was tired and needed rest. But I looked out the window and a crowd of people were coming to my front door. There were two men, Greg, Kristine and Kristine's friend plus two dogs and a cat coming across the street. I invited them in the house and after Greg introduced us. Greg seemed to stick around us and soon after we had finished some snacks. Greg went home. Grandfather mentioned going to dinner.

Greg's grandfather, Sterling, insisted so I agreed because I was free to do so. We left my house and proceeded to go across the street to his daughter's house. Then we took Sterling's friend home and got ready for the dinner. Sterling was not a big eater, but he was a good host. We had a nice steak dinner and afterwards there was dancing. We left the dance and went to a truck stop for more food.

One strange thing happened at the truck stop. A man appeared that Sterling knew and began to talk. I did not want to seem rude but it was getting rather late. So finally we left the truck stop and proceeded to my home. It was 3 AM when we reached my house.

The next day I had to go to the beauty school for a class. Sterling tried to call me and my phone number had been changed. I had forgotten about my request to have the number changed. When I got home Greg came over to ask me to call his grandfather. I called and gave him the new phone number.

My son Tommy came for a visit and while he was in town I introduced him to my new friend Sterling.

Tommy left and returned home. Sterling told me not to worry that Tommy would marry someday. He suggested a trip to San Diego or Lake Tahoe? I preferred to go to Lake Tahoe. We decided to take this trip.

We left in the camper and stopped along the way for meals at campsites. The trip was so relaxing from our regular routine. The pine trees and the Sierra Mountains are so beautiful with the glaciers all summer long. We reached Bishop, California and Sterling's relatives lived there. They were prominent citizens of that town.

We continued on our trip and came to Carson City, Nevada the capital city of the state. We rented a motel room to freshen up before meeting with Sterling's friends.

chapter twenty-six

Exciting New Venture

I just happened to have my bikini swim suit with me and it was so nice to take a dip in the pool. Sterling relaxed by the pool while I swam. After that we left and we stopped at the courthouse on the main street and obtained a marriage license. Well this was not planned so we thought what now?

It would be nice to have a ring, but on such a short decision we had no ring. We went to a cheap store and bought a set of rings that would knock your eyes out for the sum of $2.98. We found a pay phone and called Sterling's friend Shirley. When we told her that we wanted to be married she said I will arrange it.

She called back and said it was arranged for that afternoon at the Silver Dollar Saloon in Virginia City.

We arrived in Virginia City and a very small ninety year old man was there to play the old time piano in the saloon. We entered the wedding chapel and the ceremony was performed. When we came outside the chapel the little old man played Here Comes the Bride. It was no big deal.

We returned home and broke the news to our families. The news had already arrived in town and was on the radio with songs dedicated to the new bride and groom. Sterling's daughter had spread the news.

Sterling moved into my house and we rented his home. There we were right across the street from Susan his daughter. My life changed completely. The biggest change was that somebody helped me to shop for food and to carry it into the house. This job I did not like very well. We could take tours to places unknown in the state.

We could talk about our lives before we met. We exchanged tales about our families. His family became my family and my family became his. My son Tommy now had two sisters. The girls had an older brother. Most important of all I had three grandchildren and Tommy was not married yet. Thanks for small favors.

Time marched on and the grandchildren grew up to be adults. While they were growing up there were three more grandchildren born into the family. If this was not enough change Tommy got married. I had no time to feel lonely anymore.

Tommy was equally blessed when he married. He became the father of three daughters. The oldest was in college. Another daughter was a senior in high school. The youngest was a tenth grader.

Tommy had bought a home in San Jose, California. He traded his equity for a home closer to his job site. At this particular time I believe he was employed by the Intel Corporation in the Silicon Valley. He worked for that big company and later switched to the Philips Semiconductor Corporation. His home in Santa Clara was in a convenient location.

Tommy looked for another residence. They settled in San Jose in a very nice house. I was fortunate to visit them in that beautiful home.

Once there was an earthquake which shook the whole bay area. Tommy was driving on the freeway when it happened. He took the next off ramp and found the nearest gas station. Traffic lights were not working and the congestion was horrible. He was only two miles away to pick up his wife from work and naturally he was late getting there. She was frantic.

The quake had a range from Loma Prieta, in the Santa Cruz mountain area where it started, to beyond San Francisco. Highways were damaged in Oakland and the Bay Bridge had one section pulled loose where it fell on the lower deck. Many houses in San Francisco were greatly damaged. Earthquakes do not last forever and when Tommy finally showed up at her place of work they were both relieved of all the distress.

Tommy reached his home hours later found his house undisturbed but no damage except that he was without electrical power. He was exhausted and went to bed early that night. Tomorrow was another day.

Back at the home in San Jose they enjoyed the sauna bath and two patios. There were lots of shrubbery and exotic flowers outside the home. It was heaven on earth to me when I stayed a week with them.

Tommy and his wife retired from their jobs in the Silicon Valley and sold the home in San Jose. They relocated in a suburb of Santa Rosa called Rohnert Park. Tommy's youngest daughter lives just thirty miles away. She has two children who are the apple of Grandfather Tommy's eye. He makes CD's of birthday parties and other events to the delight of those grandchildren.

It was discovered a year ago that Tommy had a medical disorder. His condition was diagnosed as a herniated stomach. The surgery was performed in San Francisco at the Veterans Hospital. Tommy was informed that he had a 50-50 chance of survival.

It was really something to think about for all of us that were concerned. Tommy was in surgery eight hours and the procedure was most difficult. When the surgery was over and Tommy was taken to the recovery room, I was notified by his wife that the surgery had been successful.

For everything that happens, there is a reason and we may not know why certain things happen. Later we may see the reason. Tommy is alive and well today and we are very thankful.

Printed in the United States
by Baker & Taylor Publisher Services